Princess Chamomile's
GARDEN

Hiawyn Oram

illustrated by
Susan Varley

DUTTON CHILDREN'S BOOKS · NEW YORK

For Theo, who knows about gardens—H.O. & S.V.

31143006441837
JE Ora
Oram, Hiawyn.
Princess Chamomile's
garden
1st American ed.

CIP Data is available.

Published in the United States 2000 by Dutton Children's Books,
a division of Penguin Putnam Books for Young Readers,
345 Hudson Street, New York, New York 10014
www.penguinputnam.com
Originally published in Great Britain 2000 by Andersen Press Ltd., London
Typography by Richard Amari
Printed in Italy   First American Edition
2 4 6 8 10 9 7 5 3 1
ISBN 0-525-46387-9

Princess Chamomile was riding her bike around the kitchen gardens…
around and around and around and *around*.

"Now what shall I do?" she asked Melchior the gardener. "I can't ride around and around *forever*."

"You could help me," said Melchior.

"What, *really* help?" said Chamomile. "Really dig and really make things grow?"

"If you don't mind getting a little bit muddy."

"I don't mind getting a *lot* muddy," said Chamomile.

So Melchior found Chamomile a pitchfork that wasn't too heavy and showed her how to dig *around* the roses without digging them up and how to tell the difference between the weeds that were to be pulled and the little plants that weren't.

"Whew," she said when she'd been at it for a while. "This is *such* hard work. Maybe I'll sit in the shade for a bit."

From the shade, Chamomile looked around at the palace gardens. "The thing is," she said, "these gardens are too big. What I need is a littler, easier-to-help-in garden."

"You mean more of a your-sized garden," said Melchior.

"Yes," replied Chamomile, "and more of a my-*sort*-of garden."

"It would take planning," said Melchior. "A garden like that."

"That's okay," said Chamomile. "I'll plan it."

But at that moment Nanny Nettle arrived to fetch Chamomile for her music lesson. Nanny Nettle was not at all pleased to see dirt in Chamomile's ears and dirt under her nails and her clean-that-afternoon dress as muddy as Melchior's overalls.

She whisked her straight inside for a good scrubbing.

But Chamomile didn't care, for while Nanny Nettle and the maid scrubbed away the dirt, she was dreaming about her garden. *A good hopscotch place…* she dreamed through the washcloth.

Wildflowers for lots of butterflies… she dreamed while she played "Dance of the Sugar Plum Mice" very badly. *And a long grass place for cartwheels…*

"Excuse me, Princess," said Monsieur, her music teacher. "I think we are not concentrating today!"

"How can I concentrate?" said Chamomile. "I'm *dreaming!*"

And after her music lesson, she went on dreaming. She dreamed about her garden through supper. She dreamed about it through after-supper....

And in between Nanny Nettle coming in and out to switch off the light—and long after Nanny Nettle had finally gone to sleep—Princess Chamomile sat up in bed with paper and crayons and planned her garden halfway into the night.

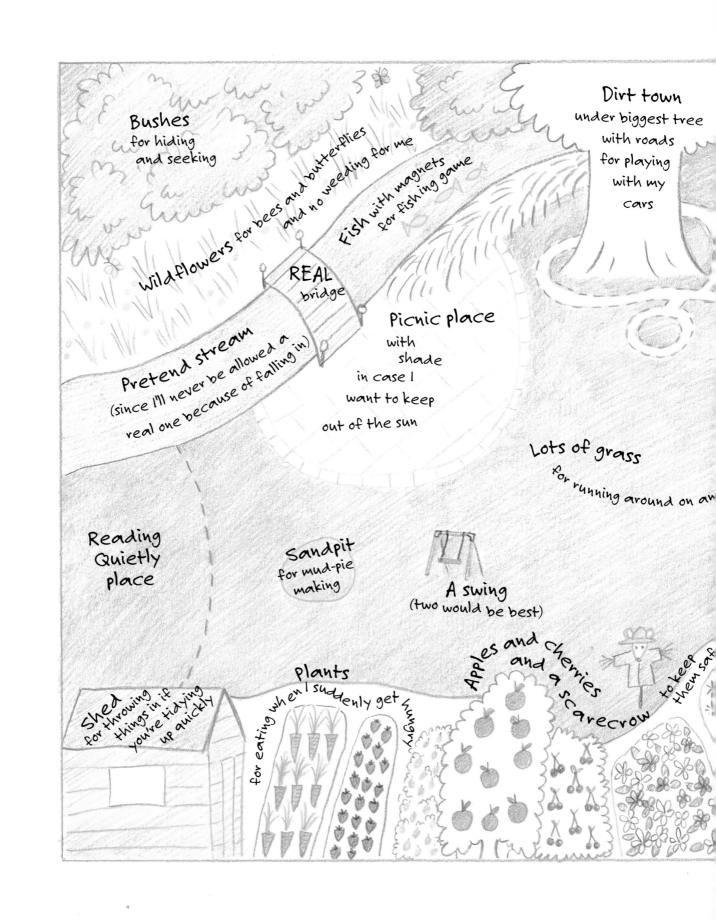

Tree house
you don't have
to climb up to because
my toys can't
climb
trees

More
hide-and-seek
bushes

Dreaming place
with flowers for looking at
—not picking

(unless there are lots)

...artwheels and playing ballgames

Gate
that's easy
for me
to open

Hopscotch
Place

Flowers for picking and giving

blue and

orange and

pink and

yellow and

red

By morning, it was ready.
This was her plan.

"What do you think?" she asked Melchior, hopping up and down.

"Hmm," said Melchior. "It won't be the smallest garden."

"It just kept growing in the plan," said Chamomile.

"Even so, it's the best your-sort-of-plan I ever saw. But before we do anything, we'll have to ask your mother and father."

Oh, please let them say yes! thought Chamomile.

But the king and queen were not at all sure.

"I don't know," the king hummed, examining the plan. "It's full of things I've never heard of in royal gardens."

"And so much long grass!" said the queen. "You'll never stop sneezing. And you'll meet so many slugs and snails!"

"That's all right," said Chamomile. "They're my friends."

"Well, I think it would spoil her rotten," said Nanny Nettle. "Her *own* sort of garden? What next! And besides, gardening is not princesslike. It's very dirty work."

"Dirt washes off," said Chamomile, "even from princesses. And I could wear big gardening clothes so that no one would even be able to tell it's me. *Please?*"

"Oh, very well," said the king, "as long as this smaller garden doesn't spoil the bigger view."

"So long as it's safe," added the queen. "And the stream *is* a pretend stream, like the one in your plan."

So, grumbling and mumbling, Nanny Nettle found Chamomile some gardening clothes…

and right then and there, without putting it off with a single "later" or "after lunch," Melchior measured out Chamomile's garden from the bigger, wider, palace-sized gardens.

Then she, Melchior, and his under-gardeners cleared
the ground...

built a wall...

trimmed the trees...

and turned over the earth.

It didn't take hours and it didn't take days. It took many long months. And as winter ended and spring began, on they worked…

sawing, cementing, hauling and hoeing; turfing, topsoiling, mulching and mowing…

potting, pricking, snipping and sowing;

weeding, watering and watching it growing.

And though *this* didn't take days but many more weeks,
suddenly, at the end of exactly the time it had taken, there
it was...Chamomile's garden according to Chamomile's plan.

And without even waiting to wash her paws, Chamomile called for the king, the queen, and Nanny Nettle, Mr. Parmesano the butler, Chervil the chauffeur, Bagley the cook, Monsieur the music teacher and the rest of the royal household to gather at the gate and admire the work.

"And by the way, you don't need to worry, Nanny Nettle," Chamomile announced. "It isn't just *my* sort of garden. It's *every-one's* sort of garden, and so you'll see…everyone's going to want to be in it!"

And she was right. They did.